Violet Mackerel's Natural Habitat

ANNA BRANFORD

illustrated by
SAM WILSON

WALKER
BOOKS

First published 2011 by Walker Books Australia Pty Ltd

First published in the UK 2013 by Walker Books Ltd
87 Vauxhall Walk, London SE11 5HJ

2 4 6 8 10 9 7 5 3 1

Text © 2011 Anna Branford
Illustrations © 2013 Sam Wilson

This book has been typeset in Bembo

Printed and bound in Great Britain by Clays Ltd, St Ives plc

British Library Cataloguing in Publication Data:
a catalogue record for this book is available from the British Library

ISBN 978-1-4063-2695-6

www.walker.co.uk

www.violetmackerel.com

To Gaynor (my mum)

AB

To Caitlin, Hannah and Kiera

SW

The Indoor Sparrow

Violet Mackerel is at the shopping centre with her mum.

It is Friday late-night shopping and they have been there for a very long time, buying violin strings for Violet's big brother Dylan, and an ENCYCLOPEDIA OF NATURAL SCIENCE for her big sister Nicola, who is doing a school project for a special **Natural Science** display. They have not been buying anything for Violet, unless you count grey school socks. Violet does not count grey school socks.

And now Mum has bumped into Mrs Lin from across the road and they are having an extremely long cup of tea in the food court.

"With petrol prices as they are," says Mum to Mrs Lin, "it's getting difficult to make ends meet."

"I know," says Mrs Lin to Mum. "My bills are going through the roof."

No one says anything to Violet, so she thinks about Mrs Lin's bills going through the roof. The roof of the food court is quite high up. Past two whole floors of shops. And there is a small brown sparrow flying there.

Violet wonders if the sparrow has always lived in the shopping centre, or if it flew in by mistake and can't find its way out of the automatic sliding doors that creak open and shut as the people come and go.

She wonders if indoor sparrows are jealous of outdoor sparrows, which have leafy trees to nest in. Or if outdoor sparrows are jealous of indoor sparrows, which get doughnut crumbs

and bits of hot dog
to eat. It is difficult to
know what small creatures
think. But while Violet is wondering,
the sparrow flies down onto the floor
of the food court and hops and jumps
just near where she is sitting.

Violet wishes she had
some doughnut crumbs,
but since she doesn't, she
tries to think of what else a
sparrow might like. She suspects it is

probably a bit difficult for an indoor sparrow to find things to build a nest with, and that gives her an idea. The hem of her daisy skirt is coming unravelled and she pulls on a loose thread. It gets quite long before it breaks. Violet puts it down on the ground for the sparrow.

"You can weave this into your nest," says Violet. The sparrow hops over, picks it up in his beak and flies back towards the roof of the shopping centre.

Violet smiles. A new thought is forming in her mind. It is called the

Theory of Finding
Small
Things

and it works like this. If you do something to help a **small thing**, that small thing might find a way of helping you. Violet quite likes helping, so she doesn't mind if the theory doesn't work. But on the other hand, it would be interesting to be helped back by something as small as a sparrow.

Violet waits to see if anything happens.

The sparrow flies back down again.

Violet wonders if it would like some more thread for its nest. This time it hops and jumps near Mrs Lin's feet.

Mrs Lin wrinkles her nose.

"Ugh, I can't stand sparrows," says Mrs Lin. "They look like mice with wings. It's time I was going home."

"Us too, I suppose," says Mum.

"Thank you," whispers Violet to the sparrow, very glad that they are finally leaving.

In the car Violet asks Mum about birds who live in shopping centres.

"Birds are good at finding places to build their nests and things to eat wherever they are," says Mum, "but a shopping centre is not a bird's **natural habitat**."

"What's a **natural habitat**?" asks Violet.

"The place where something lives and grows best," says Mum.

Violet looks up at the evening sky where the clouds are hanging low. They look as if they are about to spill their rain all over the world and she likes watching them drift in the wind. You can't see the clouds or the rain when you're in a shopping centre.

Violet suspects that the shopping centre is not her **natural habitat** either.

The Natural Science Project

When they get home, Mum and
Nicola start cooking
dinner and reading
the **ENCYCLOPEDIA
OF NATURAL
SCIENCE**
together.

ENCYCLOPEDIA
OF NATURAL

Nicola is worrying about her project. "Everyone else has something interesting for the display," Nicola is saying to Mum. "Anson McGregor is building an ant farm and Nigel Ridley is growing blue crystals and Belinda Maxwell has a real Venus flytrap plant and she will be feeding it flies with tweezers."

"Well, I'm sure you can do something interesting for your project too," says Mum. "What would you *like* to do?"

But Nicola does not know, and that is the problem. She says **Natural Science** is her worst subject. She says it is worse than Maths – much worse.

She says she does not see the *point* in rediscovering something which has already been discovered and then making a display of it.

Violet likes making displays of things, especially **small things**.

"Maybe you could discover some facts about ladybirds which *haven't* been discovered yet," says Violet. "There are lots in the garden at the moment."

"Buzz off, Violet," she says. "It's not a primary school project where you can just put some ladybirds in a jar. It is for a display and it has to be actual *science*."

"Nicola," says Mum, "Violet is only trying to help."

Violet remembers last summer when she had a cold and Nicola cheered her up by cutting big green leaves out

of paper for her to draw ladybirds on.
When she was better they did a play
about ladybirds from a story Nicola
borrowed from the library. Nicola
used to like showing Violet interesting
things and telling her good ideas. But
just lately, she seems to be grumpy
almost all of the time, especially with
Violet.

Mum says it is just a stage
and it will pass.

Violet takes a glass
jar from the kitchen
cupboard.
Nicola might
not have any ideas for herself,
but she has given one to Violet. It is
the perfect time to test the new theory
a bit more – the one about

Helping

Small

Things.

In the garden there is a patch of
fennel with soft feathery leaves and
lots of ladybirds live in it. The clouds,
which were hanging low when Violet
left the shopping centre, are starting to
drizzle rain and the ladybirds will be

getting wet. Violet wonders if it might
be helpful to make one of them a nice
dry *habitat* to stay in until the rain
stops. And it would be interesting to
see what kind of help a ladybird might
be able to give in exchange
for a cosy home
in a jar.

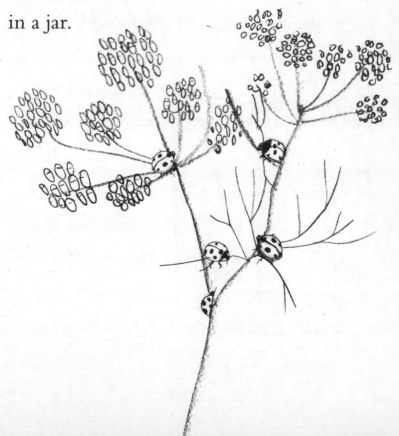

In one of the boxes in her room
Violet has some silver tinsel she saved
from Christmas, so she puts that in the
jar first. There are sweet pea flowers
in a jug on the kitchen table that
Mum's boyfriend, Vincent, gave her.
Mum doesn't mind Violet having one,
so she puts one of those in with the

tinsel. All living
creatures need
water, so Violet
sprinkles a little
bit in with her
fingertips. It is
becoming quite
a good **habitat**,
Violet thinks.

There is a particular ladybird that Violet has noticed before. The ladybird is a bit smaller than all the others and because Violet is the smallest in her family too, she feels they might share a sort of understanding. It probably has to go to bed before all the others and whenever it finds out something interesting (like that your ears keep growing all your life, even when you are old) the bigger ladybirds probably say they already knew. They might even say it a bit crossly. Violet would particularly like to give the new home she is making to that small ladybird.

She suspects the **habitat** needs one more thing. It should be something all ladybirds really like and secretly wish they had. Violet has a special wishing stone that she was given at a fairy party. It is a small, clear, rainbowy pebble and it is a particular treasure of hers. She puts it very carefully in the jar, on top of the silver tinsel but underneath the sweet pea flower. And now the new *habitat* is ready.

It is just a matter of finding the small ladybird.

The
Small Ladybird

The trouble
with **small things**
is that they can
be the hardest to
spot, especially
in the half-light
of an evening.

When Violet goes outside with her
jar and her umbrella and looks closely
into the fennel patch, at first she can't
see any ladybirds at all. Then after a
while of standing over the patch and
sheltering it with her umbrella, she can
see some of the bigger ones scurrying
about as raindrops drip through the
feathery leaves. But the small ladybird
is nowhere to be seen.

Violet looks right in the middle of
the plant, near the stalk, to see if it is
sheltering there. Then she tries looking
out at the very tips, in case it is stuck
where the leaves have been bouncing
up and down the most. She walks
in a circle around the fennel, just to

make sure she hasn't missed a spot. But she cannot find the small ladybird anywhere.

Just as she is about to give up and go back inside, she has the idea of looking among some pebbles that she and Nicola used to build a ladybird cave under the fennel leaves last summer. It was quite a secret place, which Nicola and Violet used for hiding small notes they wrote to each other, a bit like a private letterbox. That was before Nicola started going through her stage. Now the cave has fallen down, but the pebbles are still there in a little heap. Violet carefully lifts them one by one to avoid squashing any small

creature underneath. And there, right
at the bottom of the pile between two
pebbles, she spies the small ladybird.

Violet smiles.

She nudges it onto the tip of her
finger, carefully holding her umbrella
over herself and her
new friend.

"I'm Violet,"
says Violet.
"Who are
you?"

The ladybird doesn't reply, so Violet decides to give it a name. She calls it Small Gloria, which means it must be a girl. Naming a small thing is not exactly helping it, but it is a very good start, Violet thinks.

Violet inspects Small Gloria and decides she is even more beautiful close up.

She wriggles her antennae when Violet smiles at her, which might even be how a ladybird smiles. Violet is very pleased to have a new friend.

She puts her finger against the silver tinsel in the jar, and lets Small Gloria explore the new **habitat**. Small Gloria walks carefully down the tinsel and around the wishing stone, which is

nearly twenty times as big as she is.
She looks at her reflection on the side
of the glass jar for a while and then
disappears into the sweet pea.

So that Small Gloria doesn't accidentally fly out and lose her new *habitat*, Violet puts the lid on the jar. She shelters both of them under her umbrella and holds the jar very carefully when she walks, so there is not too much joggling. She takes it up to her room and places it on her bedside table.

Then it is time for dinner and it is cheese on toast. Violet saves a corner for Small Gloria.

That night, Violet says goodnight to Dylan who says goodnight back. Then she says goodnight to Nicola who doesn't say anything. Just in case,

Violet asks Nicola if she would like to
see the small ladybird from the garden,
but Nicola would not. Then Violet
says goodnight to Vincent and
to Mum and
they both
give her
a hug.

Just before bed, Violet gently opens the lid of the new **habitat** of Small Gloria. She puts in the corner of toast she has saved.

"Goodnight, Small Gloria," she says.

Violet places her ear over the opening in the top of the jar in case there is any sort of reply, but there is none.

Violet puts the lid back on, sets the jar on her bedside table and tries to go to sleep, but it is difficult when there is a new friend in your room.

In the morning it will be just her and
Nicola, since tomorrow is Saturday
and Mum and Vincent and Dylan are
all going to the markets very early.
Mum has a stall selling knitted things,
Vincent has a stall selling china birds,
and Dylan plays his violin and people
throw coins into his
violin case.

Usually, Nicola and Violet go too, so Nicola can sell the earrings she makes out of beads, and Violet can help everybody and also eat little pancakes out of a paper cup. But tomorrow Nicola will be working on her project and Violet plans to stay home too, for the pretend reason of a sleep-in, but for the *actual* reason of playing with her new friend.

The Horrible Morning

In the morning Violet has the feeling
of something exciting that you
can't quite
remember
for the first
few seconds
while you are
waking up.

And then she spies the jar on her bedside table and she remembers.

Violet picks it up and looks inside, turning it slowly and gently so that its resident doesn't get queasy. But she cannot see Small Gloria. She undoes the lid and looks inside.

Violet takes out the corner of cheese-on-toast, which does not seem very nibbled, and carefully pulls out the silver tinsel in case Small Gloria is hiding there. Then, very gently, she tweaks out the sweet pea flower.

In the
bottom of the
jar there are only two things left.

One is the wishing stone.

The other is Small Gloria, the wrong
way up and not moving, with her legs
curled tightly against her body.

Violet feels a bit queasy, as though
her **habitat** is being turned around.
The ladybird is not walking, or flying,
or even slightly moving an antenna
when Violet says "Small Gloria, are you
all right?" She is just lying still on her
back beside the wishing stone.

Violet is not sure what
to do.

It is a horrible surprise.

She sits
still on her
bed for a
little while
and wishes
Mum would come
home. She would like to
tell someone what has happened, even
though they might just say, "It's only
a ladybird" or, "It wasn't very clever
to put it in a jar". But there is only
grumpy Nicola. This morning, of all
mornings, Violet does not feel like
being buzzed off.

Violet stands in Nicola's doorway
with the jar in her hand. Nicola is
sitting at her desk still looking through
the ENCYCLOPEDIA OF NATURAL
SCIENCE. She has the look of someone
who has not been to sleep yet.

"Nicola?" says Violet.

"What?" grumps Nicola.

Violet thinks of how the problem of
Small Gloria is much more
horrible than the
problem of the
Natural Science
display, and feels
slightly cross with
Nicola, as well as
sad for herself.

Suddenly, Nicola's face goes a bit funny, like she is trying not to sneeze. Then she does a strange cough and starts crying. Nicola doesn't cry very often and when she does it is usually like a grown up, just tears and sniffling and not much noise.

This different, noisier way of crying is another bad surprise for the morning.

Violet is not supposed to go into Nicola's room without knocking and after she knocks she is supposed to wait until Nicola says, "Come in", because of an incident a few weeks ago which involved some borrowed nail polish and a spillage. But this morning, Violet just goes in and holds Nicola's hand.

"Are you crying because of your project?" asks Violet after a little while.

Nicola nods and gulps. "I can't do it," she says.

"It sounds very tricky," says Violet.

"Only to a peabrain like me," hiccups Nicola. "Everyone will laugh at me at the **Natural Science** display."

"You're not a peabrain," says Violet. "*I'm* the peabrain," she adds.

"Why are you a peabrain?" sniffs Nicola. "I tried to make a new **habitat** for Small Gloria so she wouldn't always have to be out in the cold and wet," says Violet, "and now look."

As she shows Nicola the jar with the wishing stone and the little upside-down ladybird, Violet has a lump in her throat.

Nicola does not say, "It's only a ladybird" and she also does not say, "It wasn't very clever to put it in a jar". It is nice, when someone is having a disaster, if no one says anything like that.

Violet pulls up a chair at Nicola's desk, where the **ENCYCLOPEDIA OF NATURAL SCIENCE** is still open.

"Maybe we can be peabrains together," says Violet.

The Helpful Idea

"I was reading last night about the life spans of animals," says Nicola a bit later, looking it up in the encyclopedia. "Ladybirds don't live for very long.

Mostly, the bigger the animal, the longer it lives, and the smaller the animal, the shorter it lives."

Blue whales, which are the biggest animals, can live for ninety years, reads Violet from the encyclopedia, *but mayflies, which are very tiny, live only for a few hours.*

Violet is quite glad she is a person and not a mayfly, or she would have lived all her life in the shopping centre yesterday while Mum had tea with Mrs Lin.

"How long do ladybirds live?" asks Violet.

"I'm not sure exactly," says Nicola, "but I think maybe Small Gloria would only have had a short life even if she had stayed in her *natural habitat*. I don't think it's all your fault."

Violet wishes Small Gloria was alive in the fennel patch and not dead in the bottom of a jar, but she is glad that it might not be all her fault.

"Maybe the jar was not a good *habitat* for a ladybird," says Violet.

"Maybe," says Nicola, but not meanly.

Although she still has a very big lump in her throat, Violet thinks it is nice with just the two of them, sitting at the desk in her sister's room, not being told to buzz off.

Violet looks up **ladybirds** in the encyclopedia. There is a picture of their life cycle, which starts with lots of tiny yellow eggs sitting on a leaf.

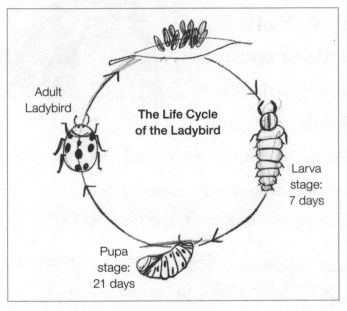

The Life Cycle
of the Ladybird

Adult
Ladybird

Larva
stage:
7 days

Pupa
stage:
21 days

They look like the little yellow seed beads Nicola sometimes uses when she is making earrings, and that gives Violet a helpful idea.

"You could make that out of green felt and yellow seed beads," she says.

Once at Christmas time, Nicola made little dangling elves with hats out of beads, and some were holding presents and some were holding candy canes.

Even though Violet helped to pack up most of the Christmas decorations, Violet quite liked the elves and still has one on

the windowsill in her
bedroom. Eggs on a
leaf are easy compared
with elves with hats
and presents.

"Everyone else has real living things
in their display," says Nicola.

"But the things you make are as
beautiful as real things," says Violet.

Nicola smiles and
says, "Thanks,
Violet."

Nicola looks thoughtfully at the encyclopedia's life cycle of the ladybird. "It would be a lot of work to make all those different stages out of beads and things," she says, sighing and slumping a little bit in her chair.

"But I could help you," says Violet.

"Thanks," says Nicola again.

Between Mum's basket of scraps, Nicola's collection of jewellery-making supplies and Violet's box of **small things**, they collect everything that they need to recreate the life cycle of the ladybird. Then they get to work. Violet holds a real leaf very still while Nicola traces around it to get its shape on the green felt. Nicola cuts it out and

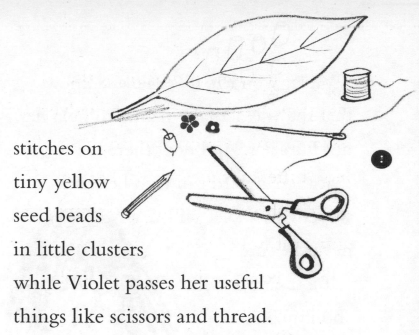

stitches on
tiny yellow
seed beads
in little clusters
while Violet passes her useful
things like scissors and thread.

Even though she is enjoying being
helpful to Nicola, Violet keeps
thinking of Small Gloria who must once
have been inside a tiny yellow egg on
a leaf. That was who Violet had most
wanted to help, and since the help
went so horribly wrong, her **Theory
of Helping Small Things** is in a slight
muddle.

Violet wonders if Small Gloria knew
that she was actually trying to help her,
not hurt her. And now there is no way
that the ladybird can help her back,
so perhaps Violet will
never be sure.

It is a sad thought
and it makes
Violet's eyes prickle
with tears.

The Red Matchbox

With Violet doing so much helping,
the first stage of the ladybird's life cycle
is ready very quickly,
but there are a lot
more stages.

 Next, using greyish–black beads, Nicola and Violet make the **larva stage**, which is when the egg becomes a long thin grub. Violet helps by carefully painting the coloured parts on, using what is left of the nail polish after the spillage.

Violet likes the **pupa stage**, which is when the larva curls up inside a kind of case. It is probably quite cosy inside a pupa, Violet thinks. Like being in a sleeping bag but with your head in too.

But the final stage is the best one. Violet reads aloud to Nicola from the **ENCYCLOPEDIA OF NATURAL SCIENCE**.

Violet wonders if it is exciting to be a newly emerging ladybird. It might be a bit like coming out of a dark movie

theatre into the busy daytime world.

Perhaps they even rub their eyes and accidentally bump into things for a little while afterwards.

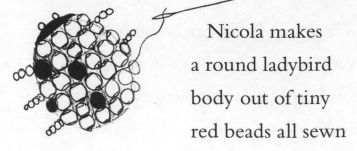

Nicola makes
a round ladybird
body out of tiny
red beads all sewn
next to each other, round and round,
spotted with black ones. This takes
the longest time of all and Violet
thinks that soon *she* may need to begin
searching for food.

Nicola has some velvet boards
that she made for when she sells her
earrings at the market. When the
beaded ladybird is finished, Violet and
Nicola pin all the different stages of the
life cycle of a ladybird onto the boards.

It is a good display and Nicola has
the look of someone who is trying

not to be too pleased in case someone thinks that it is boasting. Violet does not think it is boasting.

Violet suspects it is the most beautiful beaded life cycle of any creature that anyone has ever made.

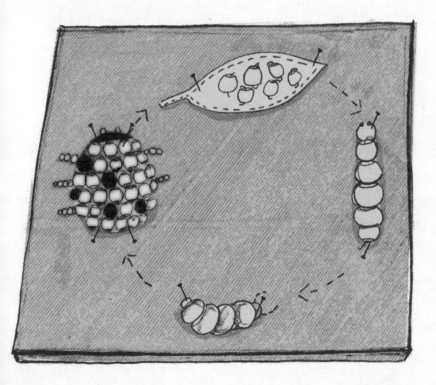

"Nicola," says Violet, "do you still need that box?" She means the matchbox which Nicola usually keeps red beads in, but now they are all used up on stage four of the ladybird life cycle, so it is empty.

"I was going to put some more beads in it," says Nicola.

"Oh," says Violet.

Even though really it is just an ordinary matchbox, Nicola has covered it in red paper and added some glitter glue and Violet likes it.

"What do you want it for?" asks Nicola.

"I need to bury

Small Gloria," says

Violet in a quiet voice. "But I'm not
sure what to bury her in."

Nicola has some scraps
of velvet left over from
when she covered the
corkboards. She folds one
into a little pillow and tucks
it inside the red matchbox.

"How's that?" she asks.

"It is perfect," says Violet.

Violet carefully tips up the jar that
was Small Gloria's home. Into her hand
fall the rainbowy glass pebble and the
round body of Small Gloria.
She lays them side
by side on the
velvet pillow.

"Where do you want to bury her?" asks Nicola.

"Under the fennel patch," says Violet. "It was her **natural habitat**."

But Violet doesn't want to bury Small Gloria just yet. She would like to think of a suitable ceremony for the burial first. So she leaves the matchbox in Nicola's room while they have lunch.

After lunch Nicola needs a nap because she didn't sleep all night from worrying about the **Natural Science** display. While Nicola is napping, Violet thinks.

Once Mum went to a funeral and when Violet asked about it afterwards, Mum said that there had been a very beautiful song that had made all the sad people feel a bit better.

So Violet goes into her room and writes a song for

Small Gloria.

The Suitable Ceremony

By the time Nicola has woken up from her nap, Violet is ready.

"I don't think Small Gloria would have wanted too much of a fuss," Violet explains to Nicola.

"But her family will all be there because they live in the fennel patch anyway. And perhaps we could say a few things and sing a song."

"You want me to come too?" asks Nicola.

"Well, even though you didn't know her, you know all about ladybirds and I think it would be nice."

"All right," says Nicola.

Violet has some red gumboots and she draws black spots on them with a marker in honour of Small Gloria.

Nicola has red spotty hairclips which Violet would like her to wear. Then they take the matchbox outside into the garden and the ceremony begins.

"I did not know Small Gloria for very long," says Violet, "but I expect that ever since she hatched, she has been a special sort of ladybird. She was my friend and I tried to help her and I didn't do a very good job. But I will remember her for ever."

Violet pauses.

"Is there anything you would like to add Nicola?"

At first Nicola cannot think of anything she would like to add. But then she says, "Actually, yes. I didn't know Small Gloria, but I am pretty sure that she knew Violet was trying to help her, not hurt her. Also, I would like to say that I am dedicating my **Natural Science** display to Small Gloria, wherever she is, because she gave a very helpful idea to Violet, and Violet gave the idea to me."

Then they sing the song which
Violet has written on a piece of paper
and it goes like this:

Flying outside
where the fennel is growing,
munching on aphids,
the breeze gently blowing
feeling the sun
on her red spotty wings,
these were a few
of small Gloria's favourite things.

Violet and Nicola bury the red matchbox in the fennel patch, together with the piece of paper with the song on it folded up. Nicola puts her arm around Violet, and Violet sends a good wish to the small ladybird.

And then it is done.

The Honourable Mention

On Monday it is the **Natural Science** display and families and friends are allowed to go and see it in the evening. So Mum, Vincent, Nicola, Dylan and Violet all go in the van to Nicola's school.

The display is set up in the school hall on tables, one for each student, and their names are on little cards at the front.

Natural Science Fair

BEAN PLANT

WAYNE KILLARNEY

There are some
very good projects,
Violet thinks. Wayne
Killarney has grown
a sort of bean plant in
special see-through
soil, so you can look
at the roots as well as

the top. Na-Kyoung Song has split the
stem of a white rose and put each half
into a different jar of water with food

colouring in it,
which has
made the
rose go half
pink and half
purple.

At the end of the evening, when
everyone has had time to look at
every single thing in the display,
there will be a prize for the Greatest
Contribution to **Natural Science**.
Violet hopes that Nicola will win it
and maybe she will, because lots of
people are stopping to look at the
beaded life cycle of the ladybird, and
one lady is saying that stages one and
two are pretty enough to wear as
a brooch.

At the bottom of Nicola's display is a little card where she has written

No eggs, larvae, pupae or ladybirds were harmed in the making of this life cycle. All creatures were left in their natural habitat.

And in very small writing on the back of the card, where no one can see, is written

In memory of Small Gloria.

It is quite exciting when the time
comes for the judging. There are three
judges and they
have all been
whispering
in a serious
way about
who will
get the prize, which is wrapped
in gold paper on their desk. Everyone
is quiet, and some of the people in
Nicola's class have their fingers crossed
 behind their backs
that they will be the
winner of whatever
is in the gold paper,
which Violet suspects

is a microscope. The only prize you get in Violet's class is a jelly bean for twenty-out-of-twenty in spelling. Violet thinks she would practise spelling more if there were prizes like microscopes to be won.

"The winner of this year's prize for the Greatest Contribution to **Natural Science**," begins the main judge, "is a student who has worked hard, thought creatively and shown a great passion for this interesting subject."

Violet is sure that Nicola has worked hard and thought creatively,

but she did
say that **Natural
Science** was worse than
Maths – much worse. Perhaps that
is not really showing a great passion.
Violet feels quite nervous.

"So we are awarding the prize to …"

Violet crosses her toes in one of her
shoes.

"Anson McGregor, for his ant farm and for his imaginative story entitled *A Day in the Life of an Ant*."

Even though Violet liked the story, she does not feel like clapping Anson McGregor. But Mum quickly says you have to clap everyone, even if they are not your sister, so Violet claps anyway, but softly and only for a short time.

When Anson McGregor opens the prize, it is not a microscope. It is only a special boxed copy of the same ENCYCLOPEDIA OF NATURAL SCIENCE that Nicola already has, which makes Violet feel a bit better about Nicola not winning it.

Then the judge says, "However, we would also like to give an Honourable Mention to Nicola Mackerel for her *Beaded Life Cycle of the Ladybird*, because it was especially made leaving all creatures in their **natural habitat**, which is the way **Natural Science** should be, wherever possible."

It is much more fun clapping Nicola, and Violet does it loudly and for quite a long time.

The judge gives Nicola an
Honourable Mention bookmark with
a tree frog on it.

And when they get home Nicola
gives it to Violet as a thank you.

The Doughnut Crumbs

Next Friday afternoon after school, Violet and Mum go to the shopping centre again as Mum needs some green wool, which is on special, and every person in the Mackerel family, plus Vincent, needs a new toothbrush.

When they
are just about to go home
they run into Mrs Lin again, who is
in the mood for a cup of tea.

"Would you mind?" Mum asks
Violet. "I know it's been a long day
already."

"I don't mind," says Violet.

So they go down to the food court.

"Please could I have a doughnut?"

asks Violet, while Mum is buying the cups of tea.

Mum says she can, and Violet picks one that is still warm and has been rolled around in cinnamon and sugar.

She eats three quarters of the doughnut and, while Mum and Mrs Lin are saying, "Aren't there a lot of advertisements on television these days" and "There is hardly any time left for the actual television shows", Violet makes the last quarter into crumbs.

The small brown sparrow flies down again. Violet thinks maybe it has remembered her because of the daisy skirt thread she gave it before.

"I have something different for you today," says Violet.

Crouching over and walking backwards very slowly, she begins to sprinkle a little trail of doughnut crumbs along the floor of the food court for the sparrow to follow. The sparrow hops and jumps along the trail, pecking at the crumbs and nibbling.

As she sprinkles, Violet thinks a bit
more about the

Theory of Helping

Small
Things

even though there isn't any particular
help she needs today.

She wonders if the sparrow might
like her to make it a soft nest in
her room, perhaps in between the
boxes of puzzles on the bookshelves.
She could listen to
it chirping in the
morning and bring
it worms from
the garden for
breakfast.

Maybe the sparrow would like to have a bath with Violet so she could shampoo its feathers while Mum shampoos Violet's hair.

Just as Violet is wondering if the sparrow might even like to come to school with her, tucked safely in her schoolbag, she finds that she has stepped onto the mat in front of the big automatic doors of the food court.

They slide open and in a flash of feathery wings, the small brown sparrow flies out.

Violet watches it flutter up into the sky and swoop over towards the park, where there are trees and a small pond and lots of other sparrows too.

HOPPING
CENTRE

Violet waves goodbye a little sadly.
It would have been fun to take the
sparrow to school.

But it is nice to think that perhaps she
has helped it find its way back to the
place it lives and grows best.

More *Violet Mackerel* stories:

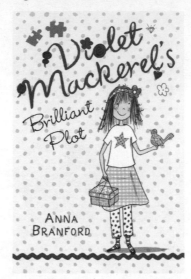

Violet thinks she would
QUITE LIKE to own the blue china
bird at the Saturday market.

This is *not* just a SILLY WISH.

It is instead the start of a
VERY IMPORTANT idea.

But what she *needs* is a PLOT.

A BRILLIANT plot...

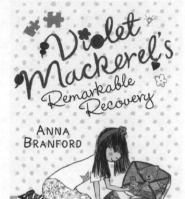

Violet has to have her tonsils out.

She does NOT think this is a good idea.

She prefers NOT to have things taken out.

But the tonsils have to go.

And that's all right, because maybe Violet will make the most REMARKABLE RECOVERY ever.

ANNA BRANFORD was born on the Isle of Man, but spent her childhood in Sudan, Papua New Guinea and Australia. Once, when she was very itchy with the chicken pox, her dad read her *The Very Hungry Caterpillar* thirty times in a row.

Anna lectures in Sociology at Victoria University, Australia, and spends her evenings writing children's stories, kept company by a furry black cat called Florence. She also makes dolls using recycled fabric and materials.

SAM WILSON graduated from Kingston University in 1999 and has since been working on lots of grown-up books. The Violet Mackerel books are the first titles she has illustrated for children. She says, "I have always wanted to illustrate for children, it has been such fun drawing Violet, she is a gorgeous character with such an adventurous spirit." Sam lives in the countryside with her husband, two children, a black Lab called Jess and several chickens.